Dynamite Doodles

doodles by:

_____

Publications International, Ltd.

S0-DVD-093

Peter Grosshauser is a doodlin' illustrator who
lives in Arizona. He's drawn for many books,
magazines, games, and comics. He also has three
children who doodle all over the house.

Illustrations: Peter Grosshauser

Doodles to Go is a trademark of Publications International, Ltd.

Louis Weber, CEO
Publications International, Ltd.
7373 North Cicero Avenue
Lincolnwood, Illinois 60712

Permission is never granted for commercial purposes.

ISBN-13: 978-1-4508-1846-9
ISBN-10: 1-4508-1846-3

Manufactured in China.

8 7 6 5 4 3 2 1

DOODLE THE DAY AWAY!

Are you a doodler? A scribbler? A sketcher? Then this is just the book for you! In fact, once you doodle your very own "Personal Property of…" stickers (project inside!), you should stick the first one on this book so no one else gets their hands on it! What's so great about this book, you ask? Our answer: What *isn't* great about this book?

Inside, you'll find tons of super cool drawings that are missing one essential ingredient: you. It's up to you and your limitless imagination to put the finishing touches on the pages in this book. Create the world's most awesome tree house. Dream up the scariest sea creature the world has ever seen. Fill a pet store with dozens of cool creatures—real or imagined. The sky is the limit! Get wild. Get crazy. It's no holds barred!

But that's not all. You'll also find easy step-by-step instructions for oodles of other doodles. A school bus, a spaceship, a dinosaur—you'll find all that and more right here.

Got a little time to spare? Our doodle projects are the perfect solution for the rainy-day blues. Maybe you want to start with the "Personal Property of…" stickers we mentioned before. Or maybe you'd like to make a gnarly surfing mobile, a masterful mask, or an awesome apron? Each project comes with a materials list that's a cinch to pull together. All the items suggested can be found in an art or craft supply shop, the grocery store, or sometimes in your own kitchen.

Instructions are as easy to follow as the materials list, but if you need an extra hand or want some good company, don't hesitate to ask an adult to join you.

Whether you like to doodle alone or in a crowd, you'll need some room to make your mark. Clear a spot at the kitchen table or at your desk and get ready to get down to business. Just be sure you lay down some newspaper if you are tackling a project that calls for glue or paint!

So what are you waiting for? There's nothing you can't "do"odle if you put your mind to it!

Doodle yourself on the day
you start this book.

I started this book on _____.

Sketch all the monsters
hiding in your bedroom.

Quick! Mom's not looking.
What will you toss in the shopping cart?

Learn to **draw**

Use the blank grid to copy the drawing.

Scary!

BOOKWORM BOOKMARK!

Are you a bookworm? Why not give these clever bookmarks a wiggle.

What You'll Need

pencil, cardstock, ruler, watercolors, paintbrush, pen, scissors, adhesive laminate

INSTRUCTIONS

1. Draw a curvy worm-like shape on the card-stock. Your worm should be about 5 inches long.

2. Use your pencil to add eyes, a smile, and a cool hat.

3. Decorate your worm with the watercolors. Add stripes, polka dots, or other fun shapes to give your worm a little extra flair.

4. Once the paint has dried, outline your worm with a pen, then cut it out.

5. Cut a 7-inch strip from your adhesive laminate and lay it on the table, sticky side up.

6. Place your worm on the adhesive laminate.

7. Cut another strip of adhesive laminate and lay it on top of your worm (sticky side down).

8. Grab your scissors and cut the adhesive laminate to the shape of your worm.

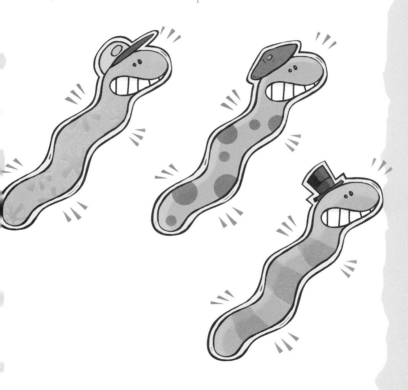

Yikes! What's that?

Yuck! What's in the soup?

STEP-BY-STEP DOODLES
UFO

Start with a half circle.

Add a frisbee below.

Then draw a bump on
the bottom.

Create your own alien to
fly the spaceship.

Now you doodle it!

Doodle your dream tree house.

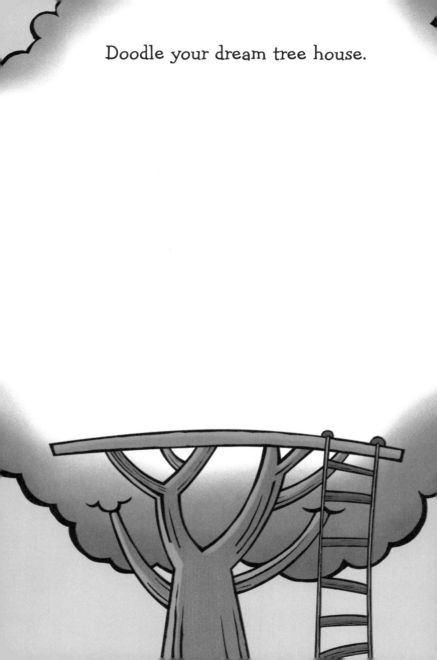

Surf's up!

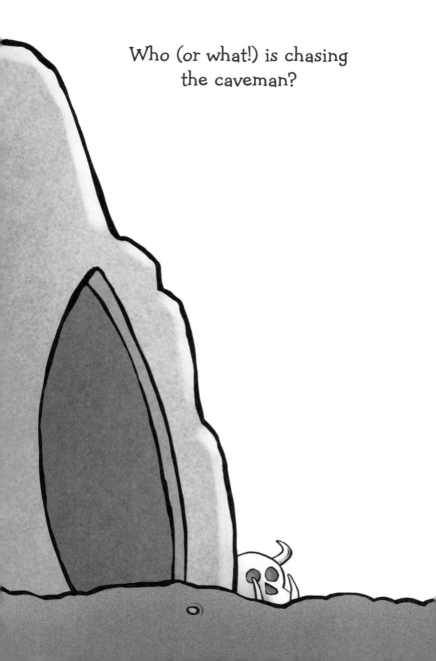

Say cheese!
What do your
photo-booth
pictures look like?
Who else is
in the picture?

Put the finishing touches on the
gingerbread house.

Learn to **draw**

Use the blank grid to copy
the drawing.

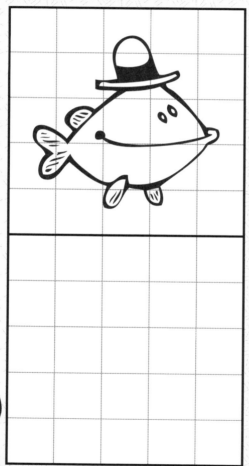

What's going on in the sewer?

HANDY ART SMOCK

Give yourself a hand for all your hard work and creativity by leaving your mark on an art smock of your very own.

What You'll Need
canvas art smock, fabric paint, applicator sponge, paintbrushes

INSTRUCTIONS

1. Prepare your work surface for painting, and lay your smock flat.

2. Use an applicator sponge to apply paint to the palm of your hand, then press your hand flat onto the smock.

3. Repeat step 2 as many times as you'd like in as many different colors as you'd like. Be sure to wash your hands when changing colors.

4. Now use your paintbrushes to doodle creative designs in between your handprints.

5. Once your handprints have dried, have fun decorating them with eyes, noses, a mouth, designs—anything you can think of.

Draw a "dino-mite" home for
these giants.

Some things are better left
buried. What's so scary?

Oh, no! You're stranded on a desert island.
What else is there with you?

STEP-BY-STEP DOODLES
PIRATE

Start with a big, wide egg shape.

Add two buck teeth to the egg.

Draw a big, thick C on the bottom...

then add two arms.

Give your pirate hands, a foot, and a peg leg.

Then draw "rabbit ears" on the side of the egg and a half circle on top of the right hand.

Draw a line across
the top half of the egg,
and add a sword on top
of the half circle.

Arrgh, Matey.
Finish your pirate
by adding your
own details.

Walk the plank by doodling your own pirate below.

Finish these faces.

Whose picture is above the fireplace?

Trick or Treat! Doodle costumes for the children.

That's quite a load! What is the ant carrying?

Learn to **draw**

Use the doodle below to get started.

Finish the doodle by adding
details and colors.

How does it work?

Invent something.

What happened to their homework?
Write or doodle their stories.

What is Jamie riding?

Yippee! This is fun!

Who is Sir George fighting?

COIN KEEPER

If you need a cool place to stash your cash,
this coin keeper makes a lot of "cents."

What You'll Need
freshly washed empty margarine container
with lid, construction paper (various colors, includ-
ing, white and red), scissors, markers, hot glue gun
(ask an adult for help!), tape measure, chenille
stem, duct tape, 2 small styrofoam spheres

INSTRUCTIONS

1. Use the lid of the margarine container to trace a circle on a piece of white construction paper and a piece of red construction paper.

2. Cut out the circles.

3. Draw some teeth on the white circle, then cut them out and glue them onto the red circle so that the edges line up.

4. Glue the red circle to the margarine lid.

5. Use the tape measure to measure the distance around the margarine container. Then measure the distance from the lip to the bottom of the container.

6. Using these measurements, draw and cut out a rectangle on construction paper.

7. Decorate this rectangle with polka dots, stripes, or flowers—whatever you like—and glue it to the container.

8. Now draw some small hands (about an inch wide) on construction paper and cut them out. Get creative! Does your monster have claws? Paws? Ten fingers on each hand?

9. Cut 2 pieces of chenille stem about 5 inches long and glue the hands to the chenille stem pieces.

10. Poke small holes on each side of the container using scissors and place a half-inch of chenille stem inside the container on either side. Use tape to secure the ends of the stems to the inside of the container.

11. Use markers to draw black circles on each of the styrofoam spheres.

12. Ask an adult to help you use a hot glue gun to secure the eyes to the container.

13. Place the lid on the container so that the teeth are on the same side as the eyes. Cut a slit in the lid and start feeding your monster coins!

NEED MORE COINS!

There's a monster in this lake!
Doodle it, then give it a name.

What's Mr. Muscle holding?

You rock! Doodle yourself as
this band's star singer.

STEP-BY-STEP DOODLES
DINOSAUR

Start with a
squiggly line.

Add another curved
line at the bottom.

Draw front legs.

Then add the
back legs.

Give your dinosaur
some eyes, a smile,
and toenails.

Now it's your turn.

What's the dog dreaming about?

Doodle a sign on the side of the city bus for all to see.

What's chasing the cat?

What is the cat chasing?

What's sweet here? Doodle delicious candy in the jars and bins.

Doodle designs on the butterflies.

PERSONAL PROPERTY STICKERS

Stuck on stickers? Now you can design and doodle cool sticker designs to label your books, CDs, and other essential gear.

What You'll Need

colored paper; scissors; colored pens, pencils, markers, or glitter gel pens; adhesive laminate; ruler

INSTRUCTIONS

1. Cut colored paper into various shapes and sizes.

2. Doodle designs on your shapes and add such messages as "Hands off!," "Property of ___," and "This belongs to___."

3. Partially peel a corner of the adhesive laminate from its backing, then slip shapes, faceup, between the sticky laminate and its backing. Make sure to leave at least a 1-inch border between shapes. Smooth laminate over the shape and backing.

4. Cut out each shape, this time making sure to leave at least a half-inch border around each one. When you're ready to use your stickers to label your stuff, simply peel off the backing!

PERSONAL PROPERTY OF:

_____

PERSONAL PROPERTY OF:

_____

It's a bird. It's a plane. No, it's a superhero here to save the day!

Abracadabra! What's that in the hat?

Doodle your royal self and
your imperial friends.

What "egg-cellent" creature is
hatching from this egg?

What's scaring the monster?

OUT OF THIS WORLD!

The only thing standing between you and the monkeys is...?

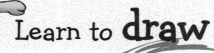

Learn to **draw**

Use the blank grid to copy
the drawing.

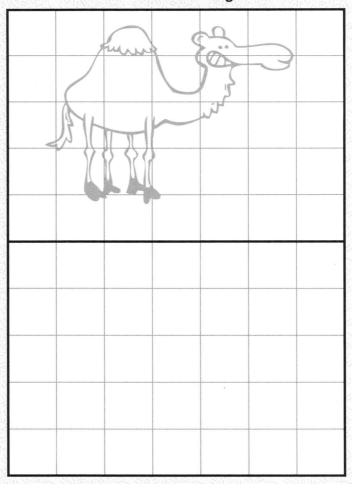

What is Chloe about to eat?

PiRATES

Ahoy, Matey! Doodle a pirate ship for this motley crew before they make you walk the plank!

Mighty fine ship we have here!

It's a jungle out here! Draw the ferocious creature that has stopped these animals in their tracks.

STEP-BY-STEP DOODLES
SCHOOL BUS

Start with a big loaf of bread.

Add a nose.

Now draw 2 big circles...

and 4 smaller circles.

Add 3 rectangles.

Finish by drawing 2 back tires.

Get on board with your own doodle!

Have a ball as you fill this jar
with things that crawl!

What's on the front of your fridge?

Who are the paparazzi following?

What's hiding in the forest?

Who is in the rocket?

Decorate the family van.

STEP-BY-STEP DOODLES
LAPTOP

Start with a
rectangle.

Add a second
rectangle...

and three more
rectangles inside
the first two.

Finish with
horizontal and
vertical lines for keys.

Now you doodle it!

What are these piranhas about
to have for lunch?

What's crawling around under the garden?

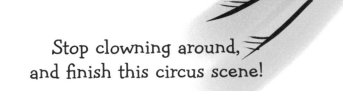

Stop clowning around,
and finish this circus scene!

DOOR HANGER

Need some peace and quiet so you can doodle to your heart's content? Design a personalized doorknob hanger so guests (and pesky little siblings) will know when you're too busy to be bothered!

What You'll Need

9×12-inch sheet of 3mm-thick craft foam, ruler, scissors, juice glass, pencil, paint pens

INSTRUCTIONS

1. Measure and cut a 4×10-inch rectangle from the craft foam.

2. Find a juice glass that's at least 3 inches in diameter (it should be slightly larger than your bedroom doorknob). Center the glass near the top of the foam rectangle, trace around the bottom of the glass, and carefully cut out the middle.

3. Use your paint pens to doodle and decorate your hanger. We've included some examples at right, but feel free to get creative with your designs! On one side, write "Genius thinking! Please don't disturb!" On the other side, write "Genius resting, do come in!"

The sky's the limit! Get creative with
your doorknob hanger doodles.

Urp! What did the snake swallow?

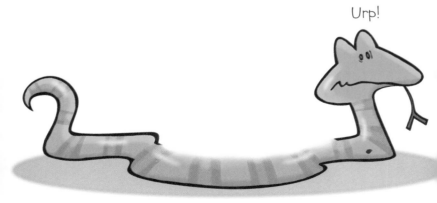

Urp!

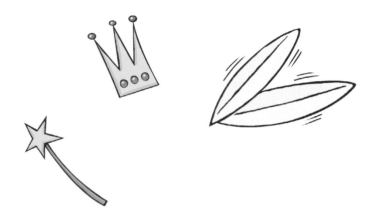

Doodle the tooth fairy of
your dreams.

You'd have a whale of a time
if you lived underwater.
Doodle your home under the sea.

Doggone it! What is the dog burying this time?

Learn to **draw**

Use the blank grid to copy the drawing.

Beautiful!

DOG PARK

Draw the pet owners to look like their dogs.

TAKE ME TO YOUR LEADER

What does the alien look like?

What is the seal balancing on its nose?

STEP-BY-STEP DOODLES
MONSTER

Draw a crooked
rectangle.

Add these
monstrous shoulders.

Draw in the mouth,
hair, ear, and collar.

Add eyes, nose, and
your favorite details.

Now it's your turn.

Design a cool roller coaster.

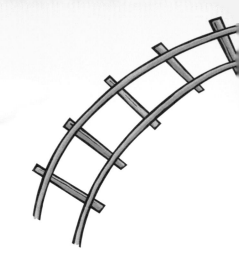

MASK-ERADE

You'll be the life of the party when you make and decorate a marvelous mask. There's no disguising the fact that you've got style!

What You'll Need

pencil, 9-inch paper plates, scissors, markers, feathers (optional), glue, hole punch, elastic cord

INSTRUCTIONS

1. Sketch eye holes on a paper plate, then use scissors to cut them out.

2. Draw a fun face on the paper plate with markers.

3. On a separate plate, cut out feathers to color.

You can also use real feathers. Glue the feathers to the back of your mask.

4. Punch a hole on each side of the mask using the hole punch.

5. Attach the elastic band through the holes and tie knots on each side to hold in place.

What's at the end of each leash?

This knight needs a castle. Draw one for him.

Learn to **draw**

Use the blank grid to copy the drawing.

Oui! Fantast

You rubbed the magic lamp and made a wish. What came out?

Doodle the animals at the pet store.

Skateboard Competition!
Doodle a slick trick.

TIMELESS TREASURES

You probably have a whole pile of stuff you're saving—ticket stubs, seashells, postcards, notes from friends. This treasure box gives you a cool place to stash it all.

What You'll Need
shoe box with lid, plain white wrapping paper, scissors, tape, markers, stickers, glitter glue

INSTRUCTIONS

1. Using the shoe box as a guide, cut two pieces of white wrapping paper so that you have one piece for the box and one piece for the lid.

2. Wrap the bottom and top of your box separately using the white wrapping paper and tape.

3. Now comes the fun part! Use your markers, stickers, glitter glue, and anything else you can find to decorate your box. Consider using old postcards, ticket stubs, or photos to make a cool collage (be sure to ask a parent first!). Finish your treasure box off with some delightful doodles of your very own!

Finish the igloo so the polar bear
has a place to keep warm.

Make the hamsters' cage the coolest around.

What's the world-famous artist painting?

What's the gorilla painting?

STEP-BY-STEP DOODLES
MP3 PLAYER

Start with a rectangle.

Draw a smaller rectangle inside the first one. Then add a circle with a smaller circle in the middle.

Doodle a squiggly line from the bottom of the rectangle.

Add circles to the ends of the squiggly lines.

Now it's your turn.

Make a splash by finishing
this waterslide.

SHARKS!

What are the sharks chasing?

SURF'S UP MOBILE!

You don't have to wait for your next vacation to relax on the beach. Capture surf and sand year-round with this awesome mobile!

What You'll Need

colored pieces of card stock, scissors, colored markers or gel pens, ruler, colored yarn or string, two 4-inch and one 8-inch wooden dowels (no more than 1/4-inch diameter), hole punch

INSTRUCTIONS

1. Cut card stock into different beach-themed shapes such as a towel, a surfboard, flip-flops, seashells, sunglasses—anything that reminds you of surf and sand.

2. Doodle decorative designs on your mobile pieces with markers.

3. Cut two 8-inch pieces of yarn or string. Tie one end of each piece to each end of the 8-inch dowel. Tie the dangling end of one string to the center of one 4-inch dowel and the dangling end of the other string to the center of the other 4-inch dowel.

4. Punch a hole in the top of each mobile piece. Tie one end of a piece of yarn or string (cut to desired length) through the hole, and tie the other end to a dowel. Note: You will have to slide the strings along the dowels until you strike the right balance. If necessary, ask a friend or grown-up for help.

5. Tie a piece of your string to the center of the 8-inch dowel, and hang the mobile above your bed.

Finish these faces.

What kind of bird is outside the window?

You're burying a time capsule so future generations can learn how cool you were. What's in it?

Time Capsule

STEP-BY-STEP DOODLES
SCOOTER

Doodle a
crooked *T*.

Add a rectangle
near the bottom
of the *T*...

and two circles
with smaller circles
inside on both ends.

Add a sideways
C over the left
circle...

then connect the
T to the rectangle
with a slanted line.

Now you doodle it!

What's your teacher eating?

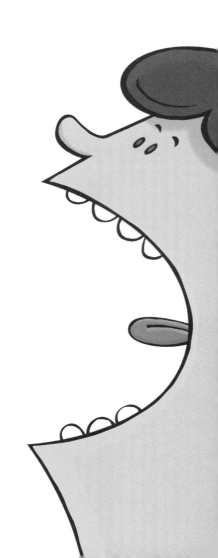

FIGHT OR FLIGHT?

You'll need to be quick to avoid the jaws of these alligators. Draw your great escape!

Looks mighty tasty!

What's playing at the movie theater?

Draw the audience's reaction to the movie.

Doodle yourself on the day
you finish this book.

I finished this book on _____.